Demystifying Men
The Blueprint

Rachel Davis

ISBN: 9781694939470

DEDICATION

I dedicate this book to the women who shaped me into the woman I am today. My Grandmother for teaching me how to be strong, my Aunt for teaching me how to know myself worth, and my Mom for teaching me how to love. I am who I am because they are who they are.

To my love, my Lover, my Warrior, my Magician, my King…Thank you for loving me the way that only you can, freely and without limitations. I dedicate my butterfly to you!!

CONTENTS

INTRODUCTION

Hello! My name is Rachel Davis. I have affectionately been given the title, Relationship Whisperer. The reason why this name has been bestowed on me is because I have been able to help countless women create better relationships with men.

A little bit about me: I have been married to the love of my life for almost a decade. We have a marriage built on solid love, trust, support, non-judgemental communication, compassion, intimacy, and safety. He makes my mind, body, and soul feel loved and safe, and that level of love, for me, is pure bliss. I look at our union as a success, because we made a vow to meet each other's needs for the rest of our lives. Knowing we wanted to keep this vow to one another, we both began to work on ourselves. For me, that is when I realized that in order to be my best self for my husband and my marriage, I needed to understand men. That is where my journey began.

The biggest aha moment for me early on in my studies was realizing that men are not the simple creatures we've always thought they are. Ladies, you heard it here first. Men are complicated! Men are equally as complex as women. You may be asking yourself, why have I never realized that before? It's because as women, we are not hardwired to understand all facets of men. We totally understand women, because we are women. However, when it comes to our male counterparts, we are often left dumbfounded by the way they think, by the way they process information, by the way they behave, and by the way they show love.

My story is quite simple. I met my husband sixteen years ago and had no idea he was going to turn my life upside down in the way that he did! It took us eight years to get married as we were much younger back then (it felt like we had all the time in the world), and we were both recently divorced when we first met. I needed time to grow and heal, and so did he. By the time we did get married, I knew I had all the ingredients to be a good wife; but, I wanted to be the *best*. I wanted to be the best at everything to ensure that I gave my marriage my all! I wanted to be a better wife to him, a better lover to him, and ultimately a better friend than I felt I had been in my previous marriage. I wanted to be the only woman he desired, mind, body, and soul!

I have been around many failed marriages in my life from immediate family members, to distant relatives, to close friends, and to distant acquaintances. I know that, ultimately, it was my responsibility to be the best me possible in my marriage and, for me to do that, I needed to understand men better. That is where my journey to demystifying men began.

This journey has been long and beautiful for me, and I have learned so much. I'm fortunate to have been personally mentored and coached by the best in the world in the study of Behavioral Reconditioning, relationships, the development of men, and so much more. I wish I could take everything that I learned and put it in the book, but that would be nearly impossible. So, I decided to take the four main archetypes of men, add elements of how they correlate to relationships with a man, and present them to you in this book.

I owe a great deal of gratitude to Robert Moore and Douglas Gillette for pioneering and spearheading the work on the archetypes of men. It is through their understanding of Carl Jung's work, the father of the archetypal theory, that this knowledge is now available. I have a great deal of gratitude for these men, for their work in laying the groundwork in deciphering the male archetype, which is the basis of this book. My heart guided me in deciding to take this path in knowing this would be the most ideal place to introduce you to my work. My true heart's desire is to allow this book to help women all across the world learn how to demystify men.

This book has indeed been a self-discovering journey for me. I learned so much about myself in this process. I learned that I am a pure perfectionist at heart and, in the process of wanting to produce something perfect for you, I realized that I needed to allow myself grace in knowing this is my first book and I can only get better from here.

I also learned that my personal vulnerability is not something I share openly and publicly. Writing this book is me opening myself and my heart to you in a vulnerable way in hopes that you are impacted by the information shared.

In closing, know that I want to give you a path that demystifies the secrets of how men think, love, and feel to provide you with the blueprint you need to help you achieve your goals in relationships with men. To start, we'll look at a case study of each archetype to give you a real-world understanding of how each type of man interacts with the world around him and to give you a sample proto-type of how his personality may have come to be. There are four main archetypes when it comes to men. Inside of every man, there is a Lover, a Warrior, a Magician, and a King. See if you recognize your ideal man in any of these men we'll closely examine! Then, we'll dive into the type of man each case study represents and examine each of his traits carefully. Ready to learn how to identify the man who will speak to your body, mind, and spirit?

Let's get started!

PART 1

The Lover

"What do you know of great love?

Have you ever loved a woman until milk leaks from her as though she had just given birth to love itself, and now must feed it or burst?

Have you ever tasted a woman until she believed that she could be satisfied only by consuming the tongue that had devoured her?

Have you ever loved a woman so completely that the sound of your voice in her ear could cause her body to shudder and explode with such intense pleasure that only weeping could bring her full release?"

— Don Juan DeMarco

Chapter One: Winston and Joan

Joan knocked gently on Winston's door. At that moment, she could feel her heart palpitating in sheer exhilaration, with anticipation of what Winston had in store for her. In her mind, Joan thought to herself how much she needed this. How much she wanted this and how much she longed for this night, longed for him.

…

Growing up in the beautiful, lush mountains of Jamaica, Winston, as a child, was full of life and energy. He was like most typical young boys raised in the islands: He loved to run in the mountains in the morning and cool off in the ocean during the evening. Winston was his mother's pride and joy. Not only was he her youngest, but he was her only son out of five children.

Growing up as a young boy, the person who had the most influence over Winston's life was his mother. Winston's father died tragically in a boating accident shortly after he was born. As a result of that loss and his Mom's inability to emotionally move on, Winston never had a strong male presence in his life to help guide him and direct him into manhood. As he got older, this was something Winston sought in men, but as a young boy, his mother was everything to him. And, because he looked so much like his father, his mother showered him with endless love and adoration, the remainder of the one true love she lost when his father passed away.

As a result of Winston being in a house as the only boy amongst six women, his mother and five sisters, he was fortunate enough to get an up-close and personal education on all things regarding women. Yet, it was Winston's relationship with his Mom that established the foundation by which he would come to expect and receive love from women.

Because Winston was the only man in the house, his Mom always found ways to make him feel special. She would prepare a special plate for him when it was time to eat dinner. Winston's Mom made sure he had space for privacy as a young man and gave him extra spending change for cake and ice cream. She always referred to him as "her little man." Each time she affectionately referred to him this way, he would be overtaken with pride and joy, knowing he played an essential role in his Mom's life. They had a deep and special bond, a bond that helped shape Winston into the man he is today.

Winston's Mom passed away shortly after his eighteenth birthday from cancer. He was hurt and angry towards God for taking away from him the one person in his life who loved him unconditionally. He agonized over her death incessantly, which caused him to slip into a space of deep despair and depression. For a long time, Winston's depression due to grieving caused him to experience extreme mood swings, sadness, and hopelessness. He wouldn't eat, he spent most of his time in bed, and he even contemplated suicide.

His sisters came together, rallied behind him, and pushed him out of the house. They encouraged him to go to England for school. This was something he and his Mom had always dreamed of for him. It was a hard decision for Winston to leave Jamaica, but he knew deep down inside that going and pursuing his education would have made his Mom happy and proud. So, he decided to take a leap of faith, left Jamaica, and relocated the U.K. to continue his education.

It didn't take long for the cloud of grieving and depression to part and expose a little bit of sunshine when he got on campus. Seeing different places and meeting new people was exactly what he needed to help him stop focusing on the passing of his one true love. Before long, Winston adjusted to his new life and started dating.

Although he met a lot of young ladies who were friendly and pleasant to be around, there was something about older women that caught his attention. He was overtaken by their confidence and found their maturity and nurturing ways intoxicating. It wasn't long before Winston began to experience women—adult women—fully. Intimately, emotionally, and sexually.

Needless to say, it did not take Winston long to become remarkably knowledgeable in the art of lovemaking. And since his palate had an unquenchable taste for mature women, it was these women who schooled him in the ways of unparalleled lovemaking. Let's just say, Winston was far more experienced than his other college-aged friends.After he finished college, Winston traveled the world and experienced all that it had to offer. He was fortunate enough to work for himself, where he did not have to be confined to a desk all day. In his travels, Winston developed a taste for fine art, fine foods, fine spirits, and fine women. He loved all things that were beautiful pleasing to his senses.After a decade of living by his own rules and experiencing all that life had to offer, he decided to relocate to the U.S., ready to settle down and feeling a strong pull toward America. It's as if his Mom's loving spirit was guiding him to relocate there. As if his future was waiting for him. He could feel it.

...

Joan was a successful attorney who worked extremely hard to get to where she was in life. You see, as a little girl, her goals and aspirations were never around getting married or having a relationship with a man. Those elements of life did not define her happiness. She was always focused on her academic wins and sports. Joan knew she had to be the best if she wanted to achieve the success she desired in life. Those were principles her mother had instilled in her from a very young age.

Growing up in a single-parent household was tough for Joan. She watched her mom struggle to give her a reliable and stable foundation, despite the fact that her father was a deadbeat. Joan's father was the poster child for letdown after letdown, disappointment after disappointment. When it came to him being there for her throughout the formative years of her life, he did not make her, nor her interests and accolades, a priority. She can remember begging her mom to call her dad because she missed him, wanted to speak to him; what a disappointing memory that turned out to be. She yearned for a man's attention, her daddy's attention. She wanted to hear him say how much he loved her and that she was beautiful, that she was his little princess, and that he was proud of her. But to no avail, he never stepped up to the plate to be the stable, sound, loving, and safe male figure she needed in her life.

Joan recalls one particular memory, her fourth grade Daddy/Daughter dance. She called her father, and it was one of those rare occasions where he actually answered. She was so excited to hear his voice on the phone that she screamed, "Daddy, Daddy, Daddy, guess what? There is a Daddy/Daughter dance at my school, and I would love for you to take me." He sounded so happy that she asked, and as she held her breath and waited for his response, he gave her a resounding, "Yes!" That "Yes" was filled with so much certainty that she knew this was going to be a special occasion for both her and her dad, one she could not wait to happen.

As the days drew near for the dance, her excitement and anticipation continued building, but what Joan did not know was that her mom had been trying for days to get in touch with her father to remind him of the dance. He did not respond to any of her calls, nor did he respond to any of her text messages. Her dad, once again, had gone MIA.

To this day, Joan can feel a lump in the back of her throat when she thinks about how hurt and disappointed she was with her father. That significant emotional event changed her view of men from that moment forward. Emotional detachment became her new best friend.

Joan began using this vice as her defense mechanism. Detaching from her emotions, when it came to her father, after experiencing that tremendous hurt and letdown came to her quickly now. Separating herself from her inner feelings enabled her to move forward, and by not giving life to her feelings, she became empowered by it. You see, her absentee "Daddy" could not hurt her anymore. As a matter of fact, no man could ever harm her in that way again.

As a successful attorney on her way to making partner in the law firm she works at, Joan does not have time. She's usually in back-to-back meetings during the day, catching up on work or taking clients out to dinner at night. Being in a relationship, getting married, or having a family is the furthest thing from her mind. Of course, she does have needs, but when it comes to men, Joan doesn't have much tolerance for the BS. She's determined to leave a situation long before any man has a chance to hurt or disappoint her.

After an extremely long day at the office, all she wanted to do was sit at the bar and enjoy her vodka tonic in peace. As she was getting ready to close her tab, the bartender grinned and told her the check had been taken care of by the gentleman across the bar. As she looked over to see who this generous sucker was, she couldn't help but be taken aback by his presence. He nodded and lifted his glass in her direction whispering, "*Salud.*"

In that instant, they locked eyes and time stood still. There was an immediate connection she could not deny. It felt like a crackle in the air, electricity vibrating around them. He, too, was able to feel what had just occurred. He felt it down to his fingertips and in his toes as he stood from his barstool and made his way towards her. With every step he took in her direction, Joan felt an intense heat radiate from her lower back and rush up towards her neck.

It was a palpable surge of energy she felt in every square inch of her body.

"My name is Winston," he said when he stood before her, with the confidence to look her square in the eye.

"I'm Joan," she replied, smiling to herself, to him.

"Is this seat taken?"

She glanced down at the barstool next to her then back up at him. "It is now."

As he sat next to her, she knew instantly her night was not about to end. He was charming, witty, charismatic, and easy to talk to. His eyes were deep and piercing. His conversation was light, free, and effortless. And he smelled delicious. Everything about him intrigued Joan, and all she knew at that very moment that she wanted more. More of his conversation, more of his gaze, more of his smile, more of his touch, more of his energy. More of everything.

...

When Winston opened the door a few weeks later, Joan immediately knew this was going to be a night she would not soon forget. Joan and Winston had gone on several dates and, each and every time they got together, she felt herself feeling more intensely for Winston. He had his ways of tapping into her senses in a very loving, safe, and sincere way. With each date, he made her feel safe in a way that began to chip away at her defenses. She began to feel again, to trust again and, to her surprise, it felt delicious.

As Winston gently interlocked his fingers with Joan's, he gently escorted her into his apartment. As she stood in front of him facing the interior of his home, he motioned behind her and gently slid her coat off. She gasped as she took it all in, the art on his walls, wooden African statues, and accents of his heritage throughout his place. He handed her a glass of Merlot, her favorite, and said, "Welcome to my home."

"Thank you!" she said as she took a moment to take him in. Winston stood about six-foot-three wearing a sheer linen shirt, fastened together only by the last button, with matching pants. She started her gaze from his deep brown eyes to the lush roundness of his full lips. She drew her eyes down to his neck and slowly over his chest. It was apparent he was putting in some overtime in the gym, because his body was amazing. Indeed, a work of art.

His apartment was dimly lit with candles as the only source of light. The light aroma of incense filled the air. Winston guided her to his sofa where they began having small talk. *How was your day? Did you eat?*

Joan was famished, which was perfect as Winston took the liberty of preparing dinner. She was thoroughly impressed with his culinary skills as she ate every morsel of food on her plate. After dinner, they made their way to the sofa to get comfortable and talk some more. The music playing in the background was both sultry and hypnotic. In an effort to make Joan wholly comfortable and relaxed, he gently slid off her shoes and began rubbing her feet. Joan looked at him and smiled as she thought to herself how wonderful it was to have someone treat her well and pay attention to her. She liked that. She liked that a lot.

After a few glasses of wine, and a couple of slow and sensual dances, they began to kiss. His kisses were long, deep, sensual, and passionate.

I don't know what it is about this man, she thought to herself.

He made her feel incredibly free and safe. Whatever was going to happen tonight, she was not going to stop it. She was ready and willing to take this as far as it could possibly go.

Amid the passion that was arising from their deep kisses, Joan unbuttoned his shirt. At that moment, Winston leaned in, gently caressed the back of her neck, and said, "I'm not going to play with your love. I'm going to introduce you to it."

...

Joan woke up the following morning being showered with butterfly kisses from the nape of her neck all the way down to the arch of her back. She'd felt waves upon waves of pure lush ecstasy the night before. Winston certainly delivered when he introduced her to all the pleasure she did not even know her body was missing.

From that day forward, they were inseparable. He showed her how beautiful life can be and how she should live it to its absolute glorious fullest. They traveled the world, experienced exotic locations, foods, wines, and people. Winston came into her dull and gray life and brought an explosion of color that only a man who is balanced and centered in Lover can genuinely deliver.

Chapter Two: The Lover Revealed

Introduction to the Lover

Welcome to the Lover archetype. I'm sure that by the mere mention of the title *Lover*, your mind will drift into thinking of all things sex-related. This archetype will have you wondering is he great in bed? Will he make my toes curl? How many ways can he make me orgasm to the point of delirium? All juicy thoughts for sure. Dating or being married to a man who leads with the Lover archetype will no doubt create an intensely romantic and highly sexual relationship. Personifying those elements are deeply rooted in a man who has fully mastered the Lover archetype; however, for the Lover to be superb at making and showing love, they must be passionate in all areas of their life not just with romance. Although the Lover takes pride in his ability to master sex and your body, there is much more than that to this archetype.

Winston has mastered the Lover archetype to its fullest. Remember, there are four main archetypes when it comes to men. Inside of every man there is a Lover, a Warrior, a Magician, and a King. A man who has a healthy balance of Love, Warrior, and Magician is worthy of being called King.

The Lover is deeply in tune with his emotions. He is not afraid of his feelings nor is he fearful of yours. He is a lover of life, family, friends, experiences, work, and passions. You name it, a Lover is passionate about it. That's why he can connect to women so easily. He is one of those men who you feel really understands you and is in tune with you. In addition to being in touch with emotions and feelings, the man who has a mature sense of his Lover temperament is a man who truly masters sensuality.

Sensuality is typically primarily reserved for all things related to having sex; however, sensuality has a broad reach when it comes to the Lover personality archetype. Being sensual, in this context, means that the Lover has a heightened and sensitive connection with their senses. A Lover will use all his senses in all areas of his life: seeing, hearing, smelling, tasting, and, most certainly, touching. It is through his senses that he experiences his world. As a woman dating a man who leads with the Lover archetype, your senses are what he will use to get you to experience him. In fact, the Lover will use sensuality in every area of his life wherever possible. And, where you both are in life will be the determining factor on whether it is a beautiful experience or painful one. We must remember that our past experiences are what ultimately make up our personalities, and how we feel about our own positions in life can also play a role in how we give and receive love.

Be mindful that the Lover archetype has a large appetite when it comes to feeding his senses. This is the archetype that drives a man's desire, even his most primal and insatiable ones, but it's also essential to remember that pleasures like sex and food are not his only driver. He also strives for a life that has meaning and purpose. Having a large appetite for pleasure is a fantastic quality in a man, especially if the man has a good, sound, and clear manifestation of the Lover archetype. His deep desires will allow him to partake in his world around him with an intense appreciation for the person that helped cultivate the pleasure he's experiencing.

The Lover is not a man only from the head up, as many men are. A Lover is a man who allows all his senses to be tantalized and is determined to ensure you experience the same pleasures as well. Being centered in this space gives life its sweetness, its connection to all things that bring pleasure to him.

The Lover has mastered the balance between giving and receiving. He maintains an awareness to both sides that supports connection and harmony. In addition to love, sex, intimacy, and everything in between, men who lead in this archetype love all things with deep and heightened sensitivity, because this archetype is the most primal one. And, since this archetype is so primal in nature for men, it will continue to play a significant role in a man's life.

His Body. The Tool.

The Lover will use his body as a tool, and, if done correctly, your body will be the instrument he enjoys fine tuning. Men whose archetype is dominated in Lover express themselves with their bodiesIf the Lover archetype is the most primal, then the primary method he uses to communicate is through his body.

Immediately after a baby is born, it's placed on its mother's bare skin. That skin-to-skin connection is a form of communication with this newborn, communicating that they are loved and safe. The use of communication through their body continues to evolve as the child gets older. For instance, babies kick, extend their arms and, of course, use their most powerful organ, the lungs, to truly express their wants and needs. Although their mind is still developing, they do not use logic, reason, or intellect to communicate. Every form of communication derives from their ability to convey their desires using their bodies.

Sensory Satisfaction

As human beings, we have all five senses: seeing, hearing, smelling, tasting and touching. There are animals in the animal kingdom that don't have all five senses, and there are others who have the same senses but heightened to a degree that defies human capacity. When it comes to humans, especially men, these senses dictate how we experience the world around us, how we interpret love, and how we give it back. The Lover archetype is about the uses of senses and its sensitivity to everything and everyone around them. They are turned on by taste, touch, hearing, smells and all things pleasing to their eyes.

To further assist you in identifying a man who leads with the Lover archetype, you should look out for the following traits:

- He enjoys all of life's pleasures, including good food, good music, drinks, art and above all, beautiful women.

- He is delighted and satisfied if he functions in a space that tantalizes all of his senses.

- He is deeply in tune with his emotions. When he's happy, he is on top of the world, but when angry or sad, he truly feels at a visceral level.

- He is deeply and spiritually connected.

- He finds inspiration in everything around him.

- He's genuinely artistic and fluid in nature.

- He loves to give pleasure.

- He loves receiving pleasure.

- He makes love to every square inch of your body as he feeds off the pleasure he's giving you.

- He listens to his intuition.

- He may not necessarily be able to keep a stable job.

- He likes being comfortable, even though being comfortable will stagnate his career/business.

- He does not want to be hurried or rushed—remember, he lives in the moment.

- He enjoys his freedom and does not easily give that up.

- He views rules as stifling and suffocating.

There are other levels to the Lover archetype that we refer to as "the shadow side." This aspect of a Lover speaks to the dangerous and sadistic side of him, which we will get into a little later.

Chapter Three: Sensory Overload

First Sense: Sight

I say this next statement with extreme confidence and absolute certainty: ALL MEN ARE VISUAL CREATURES!

In all the years I've been studying men and working with women to understand them better, I have not yet met a man who does not get turned on by the mere sight of an attractive woman. All men, but especially a man driven by the Lover archetype, will seek women who he perceives to be beautiful and will always want to have them around him. He will also be turned on visually by the parts of a woman's body that make her a woman. He will admire her breasts, her legs, her waist, her hair, her eyes, her lips and, if he has a fetish, even her feet. If he is not yet emotionally ready for a relationship, he will sample as many women as he possibly can with the sole intention of feeding his desires. Until the desire to be and love one woman comes into his awareness, the world and all the beautiful women in it are for his delight.

Second Sense: Sound

The second sense is sound. Men who are Lovers will use words to lure women in. These men have a way with words that invoke desire and intrigue in women. He knows how to use tonality to convey his passions in a way that amplifies the words coming out of his mouth. Conversely, the male Lover loves to hear how wonderful he is, how handsome he is, and much he is wanted, needed, and desired.

Third Sense: Scent

Have you ever found yourself exposed to a particular scent, a cologne perhaps, and it reminds you of someone from your past? The detail of the memory is emotionally rich in vivid detail. The reason why is that scents can take the form of heightened awareness of emotions tied to that person or experience. The power of smell is not necessarily related to an intellectual awareness or understanding; it's connected more with a felt reference point that is full of emotions. A man who leads with the Lover archetype will be drawn to all things that contain a scent reminiscent of things pleasurable in his life. So, ladies, if he expresses delight in your fragrance, continue wearing it as it can create a powerful connection with a man.

Fourth Sense: Taste

At birth, sensations in the mouth are more developed than in any other part of the body. It's no wonder why the mouth is a place of heightening sensory availability whereby bursts and explosions of passion and ecstasy can be experienced. Ever wonder why children, babies in particular, put everything in their mouth? That's because, as a baby, this is one of the main ways you learn and explore the world. For the Lover, he takes pleasure in feeling pleased with his mouth. That said, Lovers tend to be great kissers. Not only do they enjoy the act of kissing, but it also becomes an art form for them.

Fifth Sense: Touch

The man who leads with the Lover archetype has taken his time throughout his experiences with women to master the art of touch. He is a man who understands the power of touch when it comes to creating a powerful bond on all spectrums of human connections. The Lover loves to use his hands to explore life and a woman's body. He has mastered long, lingering strokes on the skin to create desire. As women, it's highly advised to use touch, as well, with the man in your life, because men are so infrequently touched. By using the softness of your hands when using non-verbal communication, it will create opportunities for him to enjoy the sensations your hands are giving him, causing him to want you and your touch more. The power of touch is not only beneficial when caressing his anatomy, but it is also equally as powerful to stroke his forearm, the nape of his neck, his chest and inner thighs.

Chapter Four: The Lover's Language

How Lover's Love

One of the most unfortunate aspects of men who do not have a healthy dose of the Lover archetype in their being is that they don't realize the capacity they have to show and give love. It's unfortunate, but the society we live in today does not allow for men to demonstrate gentle love positively and constructively. Television, movies, the entertainment and music industry, and social media alike have become the breeding ground for perpetuating toxic masculinity as the golden standard by which men are supposed to exist. Men who lead with the Lover's archetype project their capacity for love in a way that has been ridiculed and labeled as something other than manly. But, ladies, I am here to tell you, if you find a man who has a healthy dose of the Lover archetype, not just in the bedroom but in all aspects of life, love, and relationships, your emotional needs will be extremely satisfied.

Here is what you can expect when a man in the Lover archetype falls in love with you. Men show love very differently from women. One of the biggest mistakes we as women make when it comes to love and men is that we expect men to show us love in the exact same way we show love. I have no choice but to burst your bubble; having the idea that men think like us, and expecting men to act like us, is setting yourself and your relationship up for failure. Men don't think and feel like us, nor should they, not unless you want him to be the woman in your relationship. A man who is in tune with you will pay attention to you and your needs, and if he loves you and is worthy of you, he will deliver exactly what you need and want.

Acts of Love

Let's face it, ladies, most men in our society today don't function in the Lover archetype all day, every day, one hundred percent of the time. Other archetypes, which we'll get into later, like Warrior and Magician, are where most men dwell from a psychological standpoint. The Lover is oftentimes the area in his life he taps into less, because he spends most of his time working, running a business or in school and is looking for ways to achieve, excel, and dominate. So, when he is looking to conqueror and excel at life, he is NOT thinking about anything that remotely resembles being loving and gentle. That aspect is for the intimate side of his life.

So, when a man shows up for you in a powerful way by showing you the love he has for you, he is demonstrating love. I know for me, like most women, we want to hear it. We want to hear the words "I love you" every waking moment, and if he is not dominating in Lover, saying I love you all the time or saying I love you first (which is enormous for us women), may not always be his go-to method of showing love. Just in case you needed some clues on how a man shows you love in a powerful, nonverbal way, here they are:

1. He lets you into his mind and his world.

2. He introduces you to his inner circle and his family.

3. He is available to you when you need him, not only when it's convenient for him.

4. He clearly expresses his feelings for you. You do not have to guess how he feels or where you stand in his life. He will tell you.

5. He stays physically close to you because he wants to be near you. He enjoys your time and company during the day and on weekends and not just during booty-call hours.

6. He is emotionally open and available to you.

7. He apologizes even when he knows he is right. He will not allow his ego to make you feel less loved.

8. He is protective of you.

9. He is proud of you.

10. He sacrifices for you.

11. He fights for your love, even if it means clashing with himself.

12. He respects you.

13. He does things to make you happy.

14. He thinks you are beautiful even if you are at your worst.

15. He says, I love you, and means it.

Vulnerability

I want to take a moment and talk to you about vulnerability. A man in love tends to show his love carefully, especially in the beginning. He will also be extremely cautious if his trust was broken, and you both are working to reestablish it, or if he is trying to show love to a woman who he loves but who continues to emasculate him. When a man is in love, his love is projected in a nurturing and protective way. Many women miss the nurturing part, because how men nurture is very different from how women nurture.

What we, as women, desire is to have a man deeply bonded to us who makes it his life's mission to provide for and protect us and our children. With having that expectation of men, it does not leave room for men to feel safe in demonstrating vulnerability. His biggest fear is that it will be perceived as weakness.

There are parts of a man who wants to come home and be heard, held, understood, and taken care of. Because of society's standards, it is during sex that he feels most comfortable with showing vulnerability, hence one of the many reasons why sex is essential for men. Vulnerability is also tied to a man's fear of judgment and criticism. Let's face it: As women, our biggest weapon is our tongue. We can use our words to build up a man or tear him down in a heartbeat. But judgment and criticism are the quickest ways to tear down a man's confidence and cause him to close up. By allowing you and your love to be a safe haven for him, free of all the negative dogma designed to tear away at the core and essence of men, he may find his vulnerability and maybe even embrace it.

By you allowing a man to be safe and vulnerable in your love, he will love you to the end of the world. Trust me on this, he will be a better partner, husband, father, and lover.

Chapter Five: The Walk on the Dark Side

The Shadow Side of The Lover Archetype

Sex is a primal desire for men. Men live it. Breathe it. See it. Dream about it. Taste it. Smell it. Want it. They have to have it and will do just about anything to get it. There was a time where continuity of our species was dependent on it. Reproduction was the name of the game, and the males in our species were blessed with a high sex drive. Call it a gift from Mother Nature.

Fast forward to 2019. Although we have our own socio-economic and environmental ills, lack of human beings on this planet is not one of them. We are in no way in danger of being added to the endangered species list, but that desire to procreate hardwired into men's DNA does not look like it's waning anytime soon. With that in mind, growth in men occurs when they can control their sexual energy.

The force of a man's sex drive can cause him to make all sorts of decisions. Some of those decisions can be good while others can be detrimental to him, his present, and future. It is imperative that men take full control of the power of their sexual energy dwelling within the Lover archetype. If he does not take control of his sexual energy, it can create a tsunami of darkness that will not serve him in becoming a whole and balanced man.

The Addicted Lover

When the most primal of all the archetypes goes into its dark side, it can prove to be extremely destructive to the man and anyone in his path. The Addicted Lover must feed his vices. Unfortunately, those vices include, but are not limited to, the following: sex, porn, strip clubs, escorts, prostitutes, food, drugs, and alcohol. There is an intense desire for a wounded man to use any and everything that stimulates his senses to fill a void that was created. That void, in most cases, was a significant emotional event that took place early in his life. He uses these vices to produce a soothing feeling that helps to numb his pain. Some men are aware of this pain and others are utterly oblivious to the pain that is causing their destructive behavior.

I know I've stated this before, but the Lover is the most primal of the archetypes, and so, when all elements, personally and professionally that define this persona go wrong, from an addiction standpoint, it's almost as if the compulsion to give in to all of their whims shows a back-ward regression towards being barbarian like.

Examples of an Addicted Lover

Porn Addict

As previously stated, there are many vices men can become addicted to, but the one form of addiction I want to explore in this book is the addiction to porn.

Porn, like any other addiction, occurs through a process called "operant conditioning." Operant Conditioning is a process by which the method used to teach produces an outcome that is either rewarded or punished. Behavior such as watching porn creates a reinforced reaction that is directly tied to a primal act: sex brings pleasure. So, the desire to watch porn increases because it brings a reward of satisfaction each time you watch it. This is the reason why it is sometimes effortless to become addicted to porn.

To understand more of the impact porn has on men and how it influences their relationships with women, these truly mind-boggling statistics, will shed a little light for us.

According to PornHub, in 2017 alone, the site had 28.5 billion visits. That's 81 million per day, almost four million an hour, roughly 56,000 people visiting the porn site per minute. In the amount of time it takes you to read this passage, some porn sites will have received more than 100,000 visits. PornHub also states that its audience is 75% men and 25% women.

Here are a few other statistics from other resources:

- 68% of Christian men watch porn.

- 20% of men admit to watching porn online AT WORK.

- The porn industry's annual revenue is more than the NFL, NBA, and MLB combined. It is also more than the combined revenues of ABC, CBS, and NBC.

- Pornography use increases the marital infidelity rate by more than 300%.

When a man is unable to command healthy control over his Lover archetype, he can easily go left and be emotionally disruptive to himself and the person he loves. If left unchecked, it can create addictive behaviors that can impact not only his ability to truly connect with a woman and love cleanly, but also put him in a situation where he compromises his commitment to his faith. That can subsequently cost him his livelihood, his reputation, and his family.

The Impotent Lover

If the Lover archetype is centered and balanced, and the Addict Lover is far left, then the Impotent Lover is far right. An Impotent Lover is a man who is entirely limp and deflated in all aspects of the Lover archetype. He has no energy, no libido, or zest or joy for life. He is dull, stoic, and has no imagination. He is boring to his absolute core. He does not want to do anything, and lovemaking is the furthest thing from his mind. In this emotional state, he is flat, does not want to enjoy all that life has to offer, and is quite comfortable in feeling no joy.

With that being the case, when it comes to showing love through intimacy and lovemaking, he has no interest in it. He lacks interest and sexual emotions as well as sensitivity to sensuality. He may even develop depression and no longer have an interest in living life at all.

The Addicted Lover and the Impotent Lover come to life when the shadow side rears its ugly head. These issues occur when a man does not have a healthy balance of the Lover archetype in his life. Addictive behavior or an Impotent Lover quality is just the beginning. Let's take narcissism as an example. Narcissistic men will do anything to you, regardless of how much it hurts and cuts you to your core, to ease the pain of grief and lacking that eats away at their soul. Being in love with a narcissist man is one of the most painful relationships a woman could ever find herself in. Stay tuned to the next book as I will dig deeper into the Dark Side more and discuss narcissism as well as other personality defects.

In summary, the Lover is the part of a man's psyche that offers love, passion, sensuality, tenderness, compassion, sympathy, and kindness. This is an area where a lot of men feel the most vulnerable, but, in actuality, it is the most potent archetype of all of them. The men who master Lover are often the ones who make women happiest, since their goal is to offer love and pleasure; however, this is not the type of man most women will end up marrying or seeing as an ideal provider and protector. Although women say they want the kind, loving, and caring man, when it comes to husband material, she will often opt for The Warrior.

The Work

The work is a section at the conclusion of each archetype that allows you to take in what you read about the archetype and reflect on relationships you've had with a man or men who lead(s) with this archetype. Whether it's the positive side or the shadow side of his archetype, I want you to fully meditate on what you read and honor your process in growing what was shared. This page is being offered to you so that you can fully express how you feel about what you have learned and what enhancements you will make to your love life for the future.

This is your space to be honest and true to yourself. Here's a warning. Sometimes, self-discovery is not always pleasant. It can be an extremely bitter pill to swallow. But, what I can assure you of is this: If you are ready to learn and understand where you can make changes in the mistakes you have been making with the men you choose or if you come to the realization that the man in your life is truly who you want, then taking the time to do the work is priceless. Be gentle with yourself , trust your process, and know that this will take you closer to enlightenment and personal understanding.

1) After learning about the Lover, I realized...

2) What did you learn about yourself when it comes to relating to the Lover archetype in men?

3) Have you been in a relationship with a man who leads with one of the shadow sides of the Lover archetype? If yes, what clarity did you gain from this section of the book?

4) How will you better relate to men who lead with Lover?

Part 2

The Warrior

"He will not let anyone see the terrors he holds inside,
yet, he is not afraid to Cry.
He is strong for everyone else on the outside, always there
for whoever is in need.
He is a rock, he knows no Greed. So sincere in all he does.
Kindness is all his Heart knows. He is a Strong Man, the
strongest I have ever known.
Gentle is his eyes, his generosity flies. Soars beyond the
Skies.
He is real and that is rare. Positively One of a Kind.
A caring father. A respectful son. A loving lover.
A Strong Man."

- Ashley Dowdy (Forbus)

Chapter Six: William and Jessica

Jessica always knew she wanted a strong, powerful man as a husband. A man who was tall, masculine, physically built and portrayed himself as being the ideal husband who could provide for her and, more importantly, protect her. She met William and was elated at the fact that he was a police officer. Being in law enforcement, she knew he had what it took to protect her and keep her safe.

Jessica had an amazing relationship with her dad. She was the apple of his eye, and he made sure she knew it. Jessica was an only child who didn't have the pleasure of being raised by both her mother and father. Jessica's mother died while giving birth to her, and as a result of that traumatic experience for her dad, she became the center of his heart and his top priority. Jessica was undoubtedly a "Daddy's Girl" and was spoiled rotten. He never deprived her of love, affection, attention, or time. Her father, Dave, knew it was up to him to teach Jessica how she should expect to be treated by men. She remembered her father being tall and strong, and she always felt protected in his arms. He was her life, she was his, and all was right in her world.

Jessica loved it when her daddy gave her piggyback rides. As a little girl, they had a ritual every night: When it was time for bed, she would get a piggyback ride into her room. He would then proceed to tuck her in at night and read her a bedtime story. Sometimes, when her dad was up to it, he would tell her stories about her mom. He would share with her how they'd met. He took great pleasure in detailing how, on their first date, he took her mom out for ice cream. He described how they talked and ate ice cream for hours. Those were beautiful and dear memories he would share with Jessica of her mother. He freely talked about his special memories of getting to know her, falling in love with her, and plans of having a long and beautiful life together. Oftentimes, he would get sad while telling those stories about her mother, knowing it was necessary. One thing's for sure, Jessica wanted a man to love her the same way her dad loved her mom. Her father was the first man Jessica ever fell in love with, and she spent the rest of her life trying to find a man to fill her daddy's shoes.

Jessica's life got turned upside down when her father died in a tragic car accident. She was only eleven years old. Feeling lost and alone in the world, she went from having her greatest and biggest support system to now living with a distant relative she barely knew.

The premature passing of her father was a significant blow to Jessica. From that day forward, her inner light became dim, and she was never quite the same. As Jessica grew older, the one thing she knew for absolute certain was that she longed for and craved feeling loved, adored, and protected in the way her daddy had made her feel all her life. That deep hunger for love and protection caused her to make a lot of mistakes with men who weren't entirely whole and didn't have the best intentions.

…

When William came home after serving our country in Afghanistan, he knew deep within that he wasn't the same man he'd once been. The young, fearless, optimistic, energetic, fun-loving person he was before being deployed was certainly not the person he came home as.

William was very aware of the elevated levels of aggression that haunted him every day. This anger and aggression became a part of his persona as a result of all he'd been exposed to while serving his tour in Afghanistan. He knew this was some sort of post-traumatic stress syndrome, but he didn't want to fully accept it. He worked tirelessly to keep his toxic energy at bay, but he was growing tired and weary as his anger began to control his every thought and disposition with so little he could do to keep it at bay. He was a keg waiting to explode. Although he tried to deny it to himself, deep down inside, he knew it was a matter of time before he exploded and not only hurt himself but hurt the closest people to him.

After William served his four years and left the military, he found it difficult to find a job that he really wanted. There weren't too many options out there that took his skill in combat and weaponry as a resume booster, so joining the police force seemed like the most natural progression for him as it related to his career. He thoroughly enjoyed being a police officer. The guys he worked with were familiar to his spirit, which made it easy for him to form a brotherhood similar to the bond he'd formed with the men he'd served with in the war. Finally, he was in a space that allowed him to express himself authentically and provided him an opportunity to serve and protect, a personality trait embedded deep within his spirit that resonated with his identity. Beyond that, it also allowed him a space to be free to exert this pent-up aggression.

Without William seeking help for his post-traumatic stress disorder and not taking the necessary steps to get himself to a mentally healthy place, he became desensitized to his aggression and began to identify more with it. He was extremely effective in hiding his aggression from Jessica, and, when triggered, he displayed it in a way that made her feel safe and secure. There was never a moment of the day when Jessica didn't feel completely safe with him.

William and Jessica had a whirlwind love affair. They met, fell madly in love, and in less than one year were married. Jessica received a lot of opposition from her family and friends who thought she was moving too fast. The people closest to her didn't get a good vibe from William when he was around. Because he felt their discomfort with him, he started becoming more and more possessive—increasingly angry—not wanting her to have the freedom and independence of a life outside of him.

The activities William had grown accustomed to channeling his aggressions were no longer enough. Bit by bit, he began to blame Jessica for every piece of his life that hadn't fallen in line with the vision he had for himself.

It all seemed to happen so quickly that Jessica didn't notice the change turning violent until she was already on the other side of safe, in emotional and physical danger in her own home. Jessica felt trapped. She loved William, and she loved the fact that she used to feel safe and protected by him, but what she failed to realize was that the false sense of protection she received from William was a result of her compensating for the void left in her life by the absence of her father. Her hunt for a protector had turned her into the prey.

She often asked herself, *How can I still feel love for someone who abuses me? How can I want to help someone who causes me so much pain? Why am I so quick to forgive every single time he hits me simply because he gets on his knees, cries, and begs for forgiveness? Why is leaving him the hardest thing for me to do?* What she didn't realize was that William was a classic example of a Warrior archetype gone wrong.

William knew he needed help. He often hated himself when he would think back to how much he'd hurt Jessica and how often he'd made her cry. Without a doubt, he knew he truly loved her, but he also knew that if his underlying pain and rage went unaddressed, he could prove to be detrimental not only to himself but to the wellbeing and safety of the woman he loved as well.

William sought help and spent months in therapy. It was as a result of going to therapy that he was able to release the trauma and pent-up aggression he carried that stemmed from everything he did and experienced while serving in Afghanistan.

William realized that his old toxic self had to die so that he could be reborn and create space for a beautiful relationship to emerge with Jessica.

It has been some years since I've worked with William and Jessica, and I am proud to say they're doing exceptionally well. They are still madly and passionately in love with one another and have since welcomed two beautiful babies into their family. William is a classic example of a man who leads with Warrior but had a significant emotional event that caused him to slip into his shadow side. Yet, when he was willing to allow his toxic self to die, when he sought help and subsequently re-emerged as the man he desired to be, all became right in his world.

Chapter Seven: The Warrior Within

The Warrior archetype is the epitome of the persona of men. Men embody this archetype, because it comes most naturally to them. This archetype describes a man's ability and innate desire to prove his worth, provide for his family, and protect what is his. The Warrior is strong, resilient, fearless, and always willing to fight and defend what is his.

It is important to note that this archetype is how most men desire to be regarded. He wants to be the hero in all aspects of his life: at home, at work, to his spouse, to his children, and to his community. During prehistoric times, it was the Warrior archetype, deep within the male's psyche, to which we can attribute the survival of our race. It's the reason why the man had the energy and desire to hunt, kill, build, fight, survive, and tame this untamed world.

Since it was the Warrior persona that manifested itself when it became a matter of life and death, it became the very foundation that the ideal of masculinity was built upon. The Warrior archetype is the one most men resonate with and, conversely, the one women seem to be either extremely attracted to or the most uncomfortable with.

Loving A Warrior Man

Being in a relationship with a man who leads with Warrior can provide you great joy in knowing that you have a man who has your back in life. It can, however, also cause you to feel the most profound pain if he lacks the ability to show you love in a manner in which you, as a woman, desire to be loved.

If you are in a relationship with a man who leads with Warrior, there are a few perks that come with him, one of them being his extreme loyalty. Warriors, like soldiers, are loyal through and through. If they believe in you and in your relationship together, they are dedicated to it and will honor you.

Let's talk a little bit about the Warrior. Despite the story I chose to share to help level set the persona of the Warrior, the Warrior is an attribute most women admire in men; however, if they don't understand it, they can become fearful of it. Once fear sets in, a woman's defense mechanism is engaged. A woman will be tempted to use the strongest weapon she has to ward off this presumed danger: her tongue.

A woman's tongue can unleash the most hurtful and disempowering words that not only crush men but emasculate them in the process. If you have a man in your life who you love, and he clearly functions from the Warrior persona, the worst thing you can do is emasculate him.

He Is a Powerhouse of Energy

It takes an incredible amount of energy to be a man. By today's standards, even in light of the women's liberation movements, the majority of the women in our society today still expect a man to provide and protect. This desire does not in any way shape or form negate, downplay, or diminish a woman's ability to provide for herself or to protect herself. However, when a woman decides to embark on a relationship, partnership, or marriage with a man, there is a natural expectation for him to bring the power, strength, and energy men have always demonstrated since the dawn of time.

She wants her Warrior to desire courage for himself. Not only to be courageous in all areas of his life tied to achievement, she wants him to be bold in the way he demonstrates how much he loves her. One thing is for sure, for a man to show up fully and powerfully for his woman, for himself, for his occupation, and his community, it requires him to really engage his masculine energy.

When a man is able to tap into his complete and healthy manifestation of Warrior, he is provided with an energy that is undergirded with an unsurpassable power surge that fuels him and drives him to reach his goals, fight for a cause he's passionate about, and achieve greatness, thus enabling him to leave a lasting and fulfilling legacy. Even though women in today's society are successful and educated, with the capacity to earn six- and even seven-figure incomes, be CEO of a corporation, and don the title boss babe, boss chick, or any other empowering references that come to mind, she still wants the man she decides to have in her life to be fully engaged, alert, present, and vigilant. She doesn't want him to let complacency lull him into an idle state.

Boundaries, Man Caves, and More Boundaries!

The Warrior archetype is the foundation of the persona of man when it comes to providing and protecting. Knowing that to be the case, the best way a Warrior can provide safety for himself and his loved ones is to establish boundaries, territories so to speak. When a man sets limits, that is his way of ensuring protection.

Now, if we think back to the Neanderthal man, we'll realize that establishing boundaries and territories is one of the most age-old and obvious ways a male is able to articulate what is his and what is off-limits. It has always been this way, and this trait is still keenly embedded in modern-day males' psyches. By today's standards, those concepts still exist; yet, in establishing physical boundaries, the Warrior will also set boundaries around himself to confirm how people talk to him, treat him, and what he perceives to be acceptable behavior. As a means of protection for his loved ones, his children, family, friends, and his money, he establishes emotional boundaries as well as physical boundaries around them. If anyone breaches those boundaries, the Warrior in him is ready and willing to fight to protect what is his.

We understand that men today are not Neanderthals, but the establishment of boundaries is still relevant. Take, for example, his space. If you're in a relationship with a man, regardless of whether his primary archetype is Warrior, you may often hear him say that he needs his space. For some women, this is a concept that can be entirely foreign, especially if you're in the beginning stages of your relationship and you desire to spend every waking moment with him. In order for a man to be able to disconnect, decompress, and subsequently recharge, he needs to have an area in his home that he considers to be a retreat, an area that is private to him and for him only. Most of us refer to this as the "man cave."

When I first heard of the concept of a man cave, I thought it was silly. It wasn't until I got married that I realized how real the man cave is and how important it is to my husband. As a result of me better understanding men, my husband turned one of the empty bedrooms in our house into his DJ room, also known as his "man cave." The DJ room has all his sound and music equipment, and that is where he plays his music as often as he wants, as loud as he wants. That is also where he can spend time alone when he needs to get his thoughts together and needs time away. That is a way in which my husband is demonstrating boundaries; he designated space in our home that's just for him. When he's in his man cave, I don't disrupt him. When he is ready to come out, he does.

If space permits in their home, most married couples I know, have a setup where the husband has his own private domain. The need for establishing boundaries hardwired into the Warrior psyche causes him to want his own private space.

So, ladies, if your man desires to have a man cave and he retreats there every so often, know and understand he's not doing it to get away from you or the kids. The element of needing boundaries is a component of the Warrior male psyche. He was born with this desire.

A Man Who Is Disciplined Is a Man Who Leads

A man who is disciplined demonstrates confident mental strength and ironclad self-control. I've often heard people say that discipline is the essence of genius. If you think about the tremendous strides we, as a civilization, have made, and our male counterparts' contribution to those legendary achievements, we see that discipline has been at the center of it all. Even when it comes down to the male Warrior, how he shows love is an example of the discipline he uses to stay focused and love the one woman he is with.

So, let's think about it. When we think of unconditional love and compassion, there's an element of discipline that a man conveys when he chooses to put you above himself. It's easy for us always to want our needs met, and, as women, we demand that our needs are met fully. But it's important to understand that in order for certain men to be selfless in that way—to put us, our needs, and family first —he is clearly demonstrating a significant amount of discipline. Frequently, this goes unrecognized by us women.

A Warrior Knows his Potential and his Power.

This is probably one of the sexiest traits in a man for a woman. It's because women have been programmed to be attracted to men who know what they want and who are not afraid to go after it, especially when it comes to the female gender. We want a man who makes no bones about wanting us, desiring us, and pursuing us. However, as much as that is an attractive quality when it comes to us as individuals, it's also equally attractive when a man is acutely in tune with his potential and has a grounded understanding of his personal power. Let's face it, ladies: We don't want punks! We want a man who is entirely aware of his potential, who has a clear idea of who he is, who knows exactly where he's going and is not afraid to use his power to get there. It's one of the driving forces that creates attraction in us when it comes to men.

If you find yourself in a relationship with a man who knows his potential and is not afraid to execute his power, that is a beautiful place to be in. As I coach and counsel women and couples, one of the most significant issues women have with men is when they are functioning below their potential. A weak man who does not exert his power does not attract women. You don't want to be afraid of the man you are with, and you certainly don't want a man who has a false sense of power and can only recognize his power as control and abuse. This is why it's important for a man to have a balanced Warrior foundation.

Why Is He Emotionally Disengaged?

Often, a man will have to detach himself from his feelings, and, in extreme cases, his humanity, in order to get shit done. Also, emotional detachment is essential for a man to fulfill his role as a Warrior. It is necessary in order for the Warrior to create homeostasis in his life as well as in his territory. The Warrior's mind functions under the understanding that he will have to destroy something that is current in order for something new and more fruitful to take its place. Unfortunately for us, if we are in a relationship with a man who leads with Warrior and feels as though the relationship isn't taking him where he desires to be, he will end the relationship in an effort to create space and opportunity for the relationship he wants in the future. This aspect of emotional detachment does not only impact the relationships men have with women. It affects every area in his life where feelings and emotions get in the way of him achieving his desired outcome.

Let me give you an example. If you ask a man who leads with Warrior what is the most important thing to him, whether it's his work or his relationship, his time at home with his family or finding his place in the world, he will choose work and finding his place in the world. However, ladies, let me warn you that when you ask the Warrior this type of question, you should be prepared for him to lie to you simply because he knows the truth will hurt your feelings.

When you ask an emotionally disengaged man why he is emotionally disconnected, ten times out of ten his answer to you will be, "I don't know." Ladies, the unfortunate part of that response is that it's true. He honestly doesn't know. All he knows is that being emotionally tied or connected to a woman when he is not yet ready to be is something he perceives as holding him back from genuinely exploring all aspects and avenues of his Warrior persona. Until the Warrior psyche of a man feels as though he has conquered enough, there will always be an internal pull on him emotionally, mentally, and spiritually to go out and be his highest Warrior self. Women are not exempt from being conquered in this way. The Warrior attribute of a man is heavily present when he lacks maturity in relationships with women. The conqueror in him will continue to look at women as concubines until he becomes emotionally mature, whole, and complete in his Warrior state. So, ladies, please let this serve as a warning. If you meet a man or are in a relationship with a man who leads with Warrior who is not yet mature, he will seek to conquer when it comes to women. The Immature Warrior will cheat and have sex with multiple women until that urge to conquer women subsides.

He Is Willing to Die for What He Believes.

There is a Native American chant that the males would say to each other before going into battle: *Is today a good day to die?* That summarizes the mindset of a Warrior. Every single day, a man who leads with Warrior wakes up with his mind and heart structured to fight and die for what he believes in. That still holds true for men today.

It is effortless for people to group soldiers and warriors into the same category; I am here to tell you that there's a distinct and significant difference between a warrior and a soldier: A soldier will follow orders blindly, even though he may not fully be informed of the cause or mission he is about to die for. However, a warrior is convicted, aware, and passionate about his purpose and will still gladly fight and die for what *he* believes in, literally.

When you think about having the mindset of being willing to die for your purpose or beliefs, to someone who is not wired the same way a Warrior is, that could sound pretty morbid. As morbid as this sounds, this is one characteristic of the Warrior archetype I am impressed with the most. We talked about the Warrior having the mindset of getting things done when there is a task or mission at hand. But, to be willing to lay down your life for a cause is truly admirable. I'm so impressed with this trait because, when a man accepts that he is going to die, that is when he, indeed, will be capable of truly living. When death is in perspective, you live your life in perspective as well.

Some of the most powerful ways I have seen men embrace their Warrior are as follows:

- Being willing to kill elements of himself that perpetuate the fear that is holding him back and keeping him from reaching his greatest self.

- Being willing to kill aspects of his psyche and persona that manifest selfishness in relationships.

- Being willing to kill aspects of his character that cause pain, hurt, fear, and sadness in those he loves.

Being unafraid to diminish all components of himself that are toxic, limiting, and self-serving in order to die for a cause.

. So, if you're in a relationship with a mature, fully evolved Warrior, you have an amazing man in your life—one who is willing to sacrifice parts of himself that bring you pain and gain the courage needed to manifest himself as the Warrior he desires to be for you.

Chapter Eight: The Shadow Sides of the Warrior Archetype

The Bully

Now that we've had an opportunity to delve deeply into the Warrior persona, let's now focus on his shadow sides. One particular side I want to bring to your awareness is *The Bully*.

We're going to spend a little time on this particular subject, because it's near and dear to my heart, and I find that most often women mistake characteristics of a bully as demonstrations of love.

During my coaching sessions with women, we discuss in great detail how the man demonstrates his personality at the beginning stages of the dating process. In the very beginning, does he seem loving, kind, endearing? If those attributes are not coming from a genuine place, eventually those traits manifest themselves as controlling, obsessive, possessive, and jealous behaviors. Many of those negative characteristics reveal themselves in ways that are not healthy for the woman who is in a relationship with them. One classic indication is when a man exerts himself— his strength—in a way that is classified as bullying.

Bullies come in all shapes and sizes. It doesn't matter how tall or how short, how fat or how slim, how athletic or not, or even how popular he is. It's crucial for you to know and be aware that when you first meet a man, there's no way you can tell if he's a bully. It's not like he walks around with a sign on his forehead that says, "Hi, I'm a bully!" The best way to identify a bully is by observing how they act.

In the event that you're not sure if you've been with a bully, or are currently in a relationship with one, I'm going to share with you a few classic characteristics bullying men display:

- He has an insatiable need to be in control and to dominate you at all times.

- He is quick-tempered, impulsive, and you are often fearful of how he will react in that state.

- He appears to take pleasure when he knows he's causing you pain.

- He can never admit when you're right, and he finds it extremely difficult to ever see anything from your point of view.

- He refuses to take responsibility and always denies any wrongdoing on his own part.

- After he's hurt your feelings, he tells you that you are to blame for his anger and that you deserved what you got.

- He's good at talking his way out of situations and sweet talking you into forgiving him for hurting you.

- He is intolerant of differences.

- He feels superior to you and anyone you are associated with. This includes your family, friends, coworkers, fellow parishioners, etc.

- He lacks empathy and is insensitive to your feelings as well as the feelings of others.

Now that we've gone over these characteristics, I want you to take the next couple of minutes and ask yourself, have you ever been in a relationship with someone who has demonstrated these traits? If so, how did they make you feel?

I'm sure you didn't necessarily feel loved, wanted, cherished, or safe. As much as we want a man to demonstrate his Warrior traits and characteristics when it comes to protecting us and providing for us, it's also imperative for us to distinguish when his Warrior trait has gone wrong, and when he is exerting himself on you in an unsafe and toxic way.

Men who are classic bullies typically tend to target specific types of women. If a woman is outspoken, too assertive, independent, self-sufficient, and powerful in her own right, she will not likely be inclined to stick around and accept his abuse. Instead, men who are bullies often target women with the following characteristics:

* Low self-confidence

* Fearful

* Submissive/weak

* Depressed or sad

* Limited sense of humor

- Poor social skills

- Not very popular or well-known

- Has very few or no friends

- Excessive dependence on other adults

- A cultural disposition that is accepting of abusive behavior towards women

A bully may even decide to pursue and be with someone whom he envies to exert dominance over that woman, as if they are inclined to be with you so that they can break you down. Bullies always find pleasure in breaking others down so that they may feel superior over them.

If you find yourself in a relationship with a bully or an abuser (someone who violates and harms you physically, mentally, emotionally, sexually) I would encourage you to leave, POINT BLANK, PERIOD! If you're still in the process of finding your mental, emotional, and financial stability before departing from the bully, there are a few things you can do to ensure that you protect yourself when his temper flares.

- Whenever he gets excited or irrational, it's essential that you respond in a calm, rational but firm tone of voice.

- Be sure that you're utilizing your body language to communicate assertiveness in a way that shows you're not going to allow yourself to be bullied.

- Make sure that your actions and verbal responses don't provoke him if he is highly upset. To maintain your safety, I don't want you to add fuel to the fire.

If he escalates in a way that makes you feel your life and your physical wellbeing are in danger, call the police and leave immediately.

I know of too many women who suffer unnecessarily at the hands of a man who is an abuser. Sadly enough, staying can cost you your life. So, when the man has gone left in his warrior persona and becomes extremely toxic with it, that is not a situation you deserve to be in. Own your personal power and take the necessary steps to get yourself and your children, if applicable, to safety. It is imperative that you detach yourself from this man and this toxic relationship and allow yourself time to heal, so you can find the love that you truly deserve and desire for yourself.

The Coward

The polar opposite of The Bully is The Coward. As if you couldn't already guess, the Coward is a man who has had all of his power taken away from him. He doesn't show anger; he doesn't show desire; he doesn't show passion; he lives in a state of perpetual, continuous and unsubstantiated fear.

Sadly, there have been a lot of derogatory references made about men who dwell in this disempowered Warrior state. You'll hear references to men who manifest Coward as a "weakling," "a mama's boy," and even a "pussy." Men who are classified as Cowards tend to allow themselves to be used in such a way that denotes that their only motivation is people pleasing.

This disempowered shadow side occurs as a result of repressed anger directed inwards. These men who dwell in the state of Coward manifest themselves as being depressed with zero interest in anything. Men who are Cowards are unable to defend themselves in a relationship and find themselves involved with a woman who bullies them. A Coward is unable to stand firm in the face of a woman's anger.

I do want to share a word of caution with men who function within this realm: When a Coward is pushed beyond his limits, he tends to switch polarity and assert himself as a bully. When this happens, ladies, beware, because all hell will break loose.

In summary, as women, we want our men to be men. We want him to be strong. We want him to be a provider, a protector, a comforter, and a friend. In addition to providing and protecting, we also desire for him to show us love through caring. This archetype describes a man's ability and innate desire to prove his worth, provide for his family, and protect what is his. It is the foundation for most of the traits that we consider to be "masculine" and can be both a desirable and detrimental mode of his personality, depending on how it presents.

The Work

The work is a section at the conclusion of each archetype that allows you to take in what you read about the archetype and reflect on relationships you've had with a man or men who lead(s) with this archetype. Whether it's the positive side or the shadow side of his archetype, I want you to fully meditate on what you read and honor your process in growing what was shared. This page is being offered to you so that you can fully express how you feel about what you have learned and what enhancements you will make to your love life for the future.

This is your space to be honest and true to yourself. Here's a warning. Sometimes, self-discovery is not always pleasant. It can be an extremely bitter pill to swallow. But, what I can assure you of is this: If you are ready to learn and understand where you can make changes in the mistakes you have been making with the men you choose or if you come to the realization that the man in your life is truly who you want, then taking the time to do the work is priceless. Be gentle with yourself, trust your process, and know that this will take you closer to enlightenment and personal understanding.

1) After learning about the Warrior, I realized...

2). What did you learn about yourself when it comes to relating to the Warrior archetype in men?

3). Have you been in a relationship with a man who leads with one of the shadow sides of the Warrior archetype? If yes, what clarity did you gain from this section of the book?

4). How will you better relate to men who lead with the Warrior archetype in the future?

Part 3

The Magician

"The man is a success who has lived well,
laughed often, and loved much; who has gained the respect
of intelligent men and the love of little children;
who has filled his niche and accomplished his task; who
has left the world better than he found it,
whether by an improved poppy, a perfect poem, or a res-
cued soul;
who never lacked appreciation of earth's beauty or failed to
express it; who has always looked for the best in others and
given them the best he had; whose life was an inspiration;
whose memory a benediction."

—Bessie Anderson Stanley

Chapter Nine: Justin and Christine

Christine has come a long way since our first coaching session. I remember vividly when she had her first consultation with me. There was so much hurt, anger, and pain in her eyes and in her spirit, and it literally broke my heart as she shared with me everything that she'd experienced at the hands of her ex-husband.

Her self-esteem took a huge hit in her marriage, and once their marriage was over, she felt utterly lost. During our first session together, it was vital for me to get a full picture of everything that'd transpired in her marriage so that I could be fully aware of all the significant emotional events that'd brought us to that day.

Christine and her husband, Justin, were childhood sweethearts. They grew up together, lived in the same neighborhood, and went to the same school. His family knew her family, thus enabling them to be quite comfortable and extremely familiar with one another. During their high school years, they were inseparable. Wherever you saw Christine, Justin was never too far behind. He would walk her to school and carry her books; they would eat lunch together every day, study together, walk home together, and talk every evening before going to bed.

Justin was an exceptionally talented athlete and excelled in everything he did. His physique was to die for, and he was one of the most popular boys in school, which came with the territory since he played football and basketball. Christine was also quite the stunner. Not only was she an exotic beauty due to her Caribbean roots, but her added intellect, personality, and sweet disposition made her one of the most popular girls in school.

She was helplessly in love with Justin, and he was in love with her. They were like two peas in a pod, two birds of a feather, locked in the bliss of pure, genuine, and innocent love.

Senior year came around, and everything continued to be blissful between the two of them. They had ongoing conversations about their future as they both wanted to pursue their own dreams and attend a college that best suited their long-term career goals. As life would have it, she continued on to school to continue her studies in the medical field, and he decided to get a job in hopes of being able to pay for his own education.

Since the college Christine got accepted to was not close to home, they vowed to one another that no matter how far apart they were, they would always remain true to their relationship, as they had future plans to get married once she finished school. The two were obviously quite naïve about the challenges and difficulties that came with having a long-distance relationship. Yet, in spite of all the roadblocks, setbacks, breakups and makeups, they maintained their relationship, and, after the four years passed, they got married.

It was a beautiful wedding filled with love and happiness. Christine and Justin were surrounded by family and loved ones. Without a shadow of a doubt, Christine knew that she was about to embark on her happily ever after.

...

Justin had always had high hopes for himself. Being the product of a single-parent household and having witnessed his mother struggle to put food on the table, clothes on his back, and shelter over their heads, he knew as a young child that he didn't want his future children to struggle as he had.

He inevitably knew that success would come easily for him, because he was quite the intellectual. He excelled in mathematics and science, it was obvious that he had all the potential necessary to have a prosperous future. Yet, funding college was a challenge for him, and, as a result, he decided that getting a good-paying job would help him offset the expenses associated with paying for his education.

When Christine graduated from college and came home, things didn't pan out the way Justin had planned it.

Now that he was a husband with the responsibilities of paying the mortgage and contributing to the household bills, the possibility of going back to school to get his four-year degree seemed dim. Deeply frustrated with himself and his situation, he starting taking out all of his anger and frustration on Christine.

You see, being a husband and a provider to Christine wasn't something he wanted to do right away. He felt pressured by Christine and her family to get married when, in actuality, he really wanted to pursue his education so that he could have more, do more, be more, and provide more. Coming home to Christine from his dead-end job every day was a constant reminder of him not maximizing his potential. That made Justin angry, and when Justin was upset, he became abusive. By the time their marriage ended, Christine had endured so much verbal abuse that she felt empty, depleted, lackluster, and broken.

She did everything she could to make him happy, but, unbeknownst to her, his happiness, or lack thereof, had nothing to do with her. It had everything to do with Justin not reaching his maximum potential and seeing her and their marriage as the reason for his inadequacy.

Chapter Ten: Identifying the Magician

Of all four archetypes, the Magician is the most complex. The Mature Magician is a man who is grounded in his sense of self, who knows who he is and has the intellectual capacity to thrive at work and within the intellectual community. The Magician tends to be a connoisseur of knowledge and intellect. But, he can often be introverted and more focused on logical analysis of a situation than on thoughtfulness, romance and meeting your individual needs.

So, when you take into consideration being in love with a man who leads with the Magician archetype, he may not be the best match for every woman. A major challenge of being in a relationship with one is the fact that he can often come across as being a know it all. Because in his mind he has all the information and is of the ultimate level of intelligence, it can be difficult to get him to see things your way. Another area that women in a relationship with a Magician can have challenges is with how he uses the knowledge he acquires. He can be quite secretive and oftentimes can struggle with letting you in—into his mind, ideas, thoughts, dreams, and emotions. We'll delve into that a little later in the book.

Now, don't be scared off because we started with the challenges associated with the Magician archetype. Let me assure you, there are wonderful qualities associated with a man who leads with the Magician archetype as well. Keep reading, and you'll see what I am talking about.

Let's start off by level setting on who the Magician is. I know you may be thinking the Magician is a man who is able to pull a rabbit out of a hat or is a shady trickster. That's possible, depending on the man you're dealing with. But, ultimately, the Magician is clever and highly intelligent. He uses information that is either positive—where he is able to create opportunities to better the family unit—or manipulative whereby he's able to weaponize harmful information he has about you! Most women find it difficult to deal with a man like that.Much like the other archetypes, the Magician archetype has been present since the beginning of human history. Examples of men and women who've embodied the Magician archetype often become experts in their fields: advisers and counselors, sages and shamans.

The man who leads with the Magician archetype is a perpetual learner. He functions as the connection point between the wisdom of old and the knowledge of today. The Magician, in essence, is the innate intelligence of men. It is through the Magician archetype that a man is able to be creative—to take a thought from the idea stage and manifest it into a fully executed entity.

On the one hand, we're able to see how the evolution of our intelligence has helped humanity advance from the standpoint of mathematics, science, medicine, and technology. Conversely, with all of the wonderful advancements we've made on this planet, men have also used their intellect to destroy, to wage wars, and create weapons of mass destruction.

The man who leads with Magician has the ability to harness his power from an intellectual standpoint, which is essential for him when it comes to processing information. The Magician relies on interpretation and translation, communication and innovation. His reliance on all of these is the core essence of who he is as a man. A man who leads with Magician will always seek information, facts and data; this is the side that empowers him the most.

With the same ease that the Magician can create with his thoughts and words, he can easily destroy as well. The following traits will help you quickly identify whether a man leads with Magician:

- He is a problem solver.

- He finds it enjoyable creating and mastering technology.

- He uses reasoning, not emotions, at the forefront of his decision-making process.

- He is extremely introspective.

- He spends a lot of time thinking and not enough time talking.

- If it doesn't make logical sense to him, he finds it difficult to comprehend.

- He tends to be highly intellectual.

- He has a unique sense of charisma and is well received by others.

- He possesses the ability to wear many hats and tap into different abilities, often known as a jack of all trades.

Ladies, I'm sure that as you're reading this, you're playing back memories in your mind of a man you've had relations with in your past who lead with the Magician archetype. These are the types of men who spend their time and energy thinking rather than feeling. It can be challenging to create a lasting and loving bond with this type of man when he's always in his head.

The Magician's deep-seated knowledge also places him in a position where he can do extreme damage to the people around him, including the woman he loves. The Magician is the archetype of men you don't want to cross. He is the one who will use the knowledge he has acquired against you to your detriment, and he can be highly if he chooses.

One component that's extremely important for you to know about the man who leads with Magician is that you have to continually remind yourself that he is always in his head. As a result, it is often difficult to maintain a healthy and balanced relationship with him, especially if he's the type of man who makes you feel as though you're in a relationship by yourself.

The Magicians are often the worst heartbreakers on the planet, because they struggle when it comes to opening up to their partners. It doesn't matter how much you love him, it doesn't matter how much you show him you love him, it doesn't matter how much you do for him, it doesn't matter how much you sacrifice for him; if he's not willing to open his head as well as his heart to let you in, it will cause you to have all sorts of doubts when it comes to you as an individual and the role you play in the relationship. Being in love with a Magician who's not a fully matured will do a horrible number on your confidence and self-esteem.

Chapter Eleven: Inside the Magician's Hat

He Is a Thinker

When it comes to his work or his career, men who lead with the Magician archetype often excel, because he prides himself on being a source of information, knowledge, guidance, and instruction. He feels the strongest and has the most power in his professional position. He also succeeds in work environments because he can compartmentalize his feelings and solve problems with little to no emotion necessary.

Being in love or in a relationship with a man whose Magician is not fully developed takes a special kind of woman who can exercise a special kind of patience, because he's not always concerned with feelings as much as he is with the outcome of a situation. The Magician wants to work things out; however, in the process of working things out, it has to make sense in his head. So, as a woman, if you're presenting an issue or a challenge to a man who leads with Magician, it'll be quite difficult for you to be able to get through to him if you're coming from a place that's purely based on emotion and not logic.

Charisma Is his Superpower

At a party or social event, you will typically find the Magician at the back of the room, standing in the corner against the wall with a drink in his hands, observing everything that's taking place. He notices everything, sees everyone. In instances like this, he is merrily absorbing data, feeling like the most dominant and superior person in the room because he knows everything that is taking place.

As a result of the Magician acquiring data, he is able to quickly process the information in his head and use what he has learned to his best interest. With that in mind, he can be very charming, alluring, persuasive, endearing, and dangerous.

The Magician can use his knowledge of you to make you feel as though you're the only woman in the room, or, conversely, to make you feel as if you're the least important person in the room. The unfortunate part about the Magician archetype is that he's often merely observing life and not living it. This can lead to a very dull and lackluster life for the woman who's in a relationship with him, depending on her personality and her wants and needs out of life.

Chapter Twelve: The Shadow Side of the Magician Archetype

The Disempowered Magician: How Childhood Affects Him

When it comes to dishing out pain, a Magician who hasn't healed from his own emotional wounds, whatever they may be, is exceptionally good at it doling out hurt to your heart's detriment.

Emotional wounds in the Magician archetype tend to start in his childhood. Growing up, he may have always been told that something is wrong with him. He may have grown up in a household that did not offer constant and consistent love and reassurance, which can create emotional scars and wounds that manifest themselves in an ugly way for young boys in adulthood. So for instance, if a young boy grows up continuously hearing how different he is, or how evil he is, or the classic, "You're just like your father," accusation—especially if he does not have a good relationship with his father—this can create gaping holes and pathways for the Magician to not fully develop in a healthy way.

So, ladies, if you have a son or sons, it's crucial not to use words such as those against him or around him, no matter how angry or frustrated you may get. This is important because if he's always hearing how he doesn't measure up, he'll surely grow up feeling inferior and inadequate. Those words are like planted seeds that will manifest themselves in his adulthood as hurt. Unfortunately, those hurtful words will subsequently shape his disempowered demeanor as a man. He will eventually become comfortable with being inferior and inadequate, and if you've ever been involved with a man who did not own his sense of self, you know how painful it is to witness. If we don't change how we speak to our boys, they will grow up and become adults who walk around saying, "I'm useless; I am bad; I can't do this; I am worthless; no one loves me; no one wants me."

Now, you may be saying to yourself that if he's a strong young man then he won't internalize these thoughts, and they'll never manifest as signs of weakness. But I'm here to tell you nothing could be further from the truth. The reason men and women absorb these types of disempowering beliefs and energy is because of shame. Ladies, I hate to say it, but shame is very real, and it doesn't just impact women; it affects men as well. Shame is like a poison that destroys the very essence of good that lies within a person. It's important to know that shame can hide itself in the body and mind of a man for decades before finally manifesting itself negatively.

The Disempowered Magician: How Adolescent Shame Affects Him

I recently had a conversation with a longtime friend of the family who happens to be a Youth Minister at a local church, and he shared with me information he learned at a conference he attended. We were speaking about shame and Christianity, and what he shared with me, albeit shocking, made perfect sense when you take into account the trauma young men who suffer from publicized humiliation have been dealing with for years.

He noted that shame exists in a lot of families, especially those who are devout and extremist in their faith; particularly Christians. I know this topic may be controversial, but it certainly is food for thought. As a child who grew up in a household that was extreme in the application of biblical principles—notice I said *extreme* —I can attest that such an upbringing establishes the bedrock for a child to grow up feeling substandard. When you are told over and over again that you were born from sin and not fit to be in the presence of God because of it it can deeply manifest a sense of inadequacy that is detrimental to the child for the rest of their lives. If the child never feels adequate, clean, and sin-free enough to be in the presence of God, it sends the message that people are sinful simply because they were born and that this sin condemns them to damnation unless they're baptized or in other ways enabled to ritually shed their sins.

As human beings, we're born with sexual needs, urges, and desires. Those same needs, urges, and desires are the triggers that allow us to move toward growing and understanding the art of demonstrating love through making love. Sex represents many things to many people. It can be beautiful, earth-shattering, and blissfully erotic. It can also be painful, demeaning, dirty, perverted, or unsatisfying. A young man's introduction to sex, along with his personal sexual experiences from childhood to adulthood, shapes how he views and responds to all things sexual in nature. So, when a young man is demonized and made to feel less than human because of religious dogma (when he is simply showing curiosity about the urges he's being introduced to) he can be burdened with shame, if not nurtured in a safe environment, when he is, in fact, only curious about being human. That lack of understanding from his parents is a heavy burden to bear, especially if the young man was raised in an extreme environment that perpetuated this concept and made him feel dirty for having natural thoughts and urges that happen naturally as we come of age.

Now, I don't claim to be somebody who's centered and knowledgeable enough to speak from a faith perspective; however, I can see how, in extreme circumstances, this concept can create gaps in our young men's minds. It can manifest by evolving him into a disempowered adult carrying a heavy burden of shame as he gets older.

The Manipulator

The Manipulator is the Magician gone bad. This particular shadow energy is often referred to as the Predator. Men who don't fully evolve and fully develop into a healthy Magician often veer left and end up being a quintessential womanizer. If you've ever been in a relationship with a Manipulator, you know that it's undoubtedly a cruel situation to be in.

The Manipulator Magician is often a narcissist. The Manipulator is the essence of a man who hasn't healthily evolved into the Magician archetype. He has an emotional detachment that reveals itself as cynicism. He will exploit the information he's gathered on your vulnerabilities and victimize himself to people outside of the relationship to show himself in a better light. Manipulators do this so they can get people to see from their perspective and label you as the evil one. Unfortunately, people outside of your relationship won't know the truth of his manipulative ways and may even tend to believe his side of the story. He will also deliberately insert cruelty into the way he treats you. Cruelty can manifest itself in so many ways when you're dealing with a man who is a Manipulator. For instance, it may display as lack of sympathy and empathy, lying behaviorisms, a secretive nature, cheating tendencies, arrogance, self absorption, egotism, and/or controlling emotionally and physically abusiveness. He will likely even derive pleasure from inflicting physical pain on you. This side of the Manipulator Magician is the most extreme form, and, if gone untreated, he can evolve into a psychopath or an individual who is completely detached from humanity and emotions.

You may be asking yourself, "Well, what exactly causes a Magician to go left?" One word: fear. Deep and profound fear is the number one reason why a man who leads with Magician would engage in and find comfort in his dark side.

Let's talk about fear for a bit. A healthy form of fear can protect us from danger. It allows us to be more aware of threats around us, which, in most cases, protects us from the unknown. However, in the case of a man who uses the dark side of Magician, he is afraid of others' use of knowledge that he has against him, using it like a weapon. As opposed to allowing you to disarm him by placing the element of fear in his mind, he will instead reverse it and put that element of fear in you, utilizing your anxiety, as well as the information he has obtained about you, as a weapon to manipulate you before you can manipulate him.

The Lazy One

This deflated form of Magician, the Lazy One, is a man who adopts the passive polarity of the Magician archetype. This is a man who manifests himself as a fool, also referred to as "a simple one." Whereas the healthily manifested Magician is sure of himself because of his unquestionable knowledge of and logical approach to any given situation, the Lazy One is often confused about who he is and what he wants out of life. This archetype is deflated, because it is the embodiment of powerlessness. The Lazy One is the man who avoids taking responsibility for himself so that he can evade taking responsibility for the role he plays in your life. This shadow side is extremely passive and can be characterized as a man who lacks energy, effort, power, and, subsequently, lacks a real presence in the world.

Although this is a lazy and passive shadow side, it can show itself as being manipulative as well, because this is the shadow persona a man embodies as a result of having information. So, the element of acquiring data and information still exists within this shadow of the Magician, however, because he's so deflated and disempowered, he'd rather not act on the information. Instead, he presents himself as being completely apathetic or innocent or not very forthcoming with the knowledge and information he has, which can be seen as manipulative.

The Lazy One wants the power, the glory, and the status, but he is unwilling to work for it. He has goals, but when he is faced with putting action to those goals, if difficult, he will quit. Because of his inability to reach his aspirations, he doesn't want you to reach yours either and will do everything he can to keep you immobile toward your goals and desires. That way, you don't grow too far away from him, and you both can be in the same place together. If you're in a relationship with a man who functions as the Lazy One, he will be a stumbling block for your dreams, goals, passions, and ambitions. He will always downplay other people and their success with his inferior posture and his inferior presence. Eventually, envy sets in for him. When that happens, if directed toward you, that is a complicated relationship to be a part of—one that may warrant you reconsidering if this union is for you.

Working with Christine and helping her truly understand the Magician archetype proved to be a significant breakthrough for her. When she realized she had nothing to do with Justin's unhappiness and that his woes were a direct result of him not manifesting himself fully in his Magician archetype, she was able to free herself from all the hurt and pain she'd internalized.

The divorce had nothing to do with what Christine did or didn't do, said or didn't say. It was not a situation that came to be because she didn't fully show up for him as a wife. The crux of the issue that occurred in their marriage was that Justin needed to become his highest self in order for him to feel that he'd reached his full masculinity, something that he wasn't able to do while in the marriage.

Since their divorce, he's been able to enroll in school, graduate with a degree at the top of his class and is now experiencing the success he'd always desired for his life. A few short years and many coaching sessions later, Christine and Justin are now friends. Christine is fully empowered in her own sense of self and is better equipped to identify men who have not fully evolved into their highest self. As a result of Christine being empowered with the information I'm sharing in this book, she has since remarried and is madly in love with her husband who is also madly in love with her.

In wrapping up the Magician, you can tell there's nothing simple about this archetype. Awareness inside knowledge is at the very core of what fuels the Magician archetype in a man. In the healthy manifestation, he understands that knowledge and wisdom are powerful, and he relishes the idea of being able to be powerful in that way. As a result, he can be very persuasive, manipulative and endearing in the process, depending on how his Magician presents itself.

Much like the Lover and the Warrior, the Magician resides in every man, and when he can manifest his Magician at its fullest healthy potential, it's an amazing energy to witness. The men who come into their own in the archetype of Magician are the men who can improve the world in a way that only a powerful and intellectually grounded man can.

The Work

The work is a section at the conclusion of each archetype that allows you to take in what you read about the archetype and reflect on relationships you've had with a man or men who lead(s) with this archetype. Whether it's the positive side or the shadow side of his archetype, I want you to fully meditate on what you read and honor your process in growing what was shared. This page is being offered to you so that you can fully express how you feel about what you have learned and what enhancements you will make to your love life for the future.

This is your space to be honest and true to yourself. Here's a warning. Sometimes, self-discovery is not always pleasant. It can be an extremely bitter pill to swallow. But, what I can assure you of is this: If you are ready to learn and understand where you can make changes in the mistakes you have been making with the men you choose or if you come to the realization that the man in your life is truly who you want, then taking the time to do the work is priceless. Be gentle with yourself, trust your process, and know that this will take you closer to enlightenment and personal understanding.

1) After learning about the Magician, I realized...

2). What did you learn about yourself when it comes to relating to the Magician archetype in men?

3). Have you been in a relationship with a man who leads with one of the shadow sides of the Magician archetype? If yes, what clarity did you gain from this section of the book?

4). How will you better relate to men who lead with the Magician archetype?

Part 4

Sovereign Archetype in Men

The King

"The sacred masculine is not a look, an age, a body or a type.
It is the ability to be present of body and heart, to be open in spirit and feeling, free in soul and mind.
It is kindness merging with strength, passion blending with purpose, sexuality joining with expression, emotion meeting truth and imagination combining with intelligence.
He does not hide from what his heart speaks; he listens with open ear embracing his intuition, knowing that as warrior his instincts are sharp.
He does not run from conflict, knowing that resolution is the traits of Kings.
He will not wall off his heart from the Divine Feminine, feeling that within the flow of her love is eternity.
The sacred masculine is a force of nature and as a part of nature, has a reverence for the natural world and all the

creatures in it. His power is purposeful but not harmful, and wields a double-edged sword of strength and compassion in equal measure.

His love is a sacred space for himself to grow alone and with a companion in a place of trust, respect and soul connection. He would never lessen another to make himself more.

He is a man that acknowledges his desires, his dreams, his medicine and his deep emotions.

He needs no lineage to be crowned King."

—Ara Campbell

Chapter Thirteen: A World in Need Needs a King, Indeed

When I first heard the term "sovereign," I had to look it up in the dictionary. I'd heard references made about kings and queens, but never about sovereigns. I wanted to fully understand the technical definition in the context of these four archetypes. The following statement is what Google dictionary has listed for Sovereign:

Supreme ruler, a monarch. When used as an adjective, it's; possessing supreme or ultimate power.

I thought that was a broad yet comprehensive definition to describe Sovereign or, in this case, the King.

Before we go any further, I want to make a clear distinction: When we are referencing Sovereign in this book, it is in direct correlation to the male archetype "King." This reference, if fully realized in the feminine, would be referred to as Queen. We will delve into the female archetypes in the next book.

So, you may be saying, "Rachel, I know what a king is. I've learned all about kings throughout history, and I'm fully aware of the role the king plays in society, both past and present." You may even be saying to yourself, "I have a man in my life, and he is the king of my world." Alternatively, if you have an amazingly beautiful relationship with your dad, you may say your dad has King-like qualities that you desire to have in your future husband.

Well, ladies, I'm here to tell you the King archetype is all of that and so much more.

Let's talk a little bit about the purpose of a king. As I began to delve in and intensely study the science and psychology that produced the archetypes through the teaching of Robert Moore, a psychoanalytic scientist, and Douglas Gillette, a psychologist, who were students of C.G. Jung, there was one aspect of the King that stood out to me above all other components used to characterize this persona. That is that the purpose of the King is to be a divine channel in which goodness and prosperity can flow through the people around him and the people he serves. That divine channel of goodness and prosperity that flows through him is God!

When I read that, I was like, "Whoa!" That one sentence made me take an introspective look at all the men that entered my life, as well as all who have exited, my life as a child. As I reflected on them, I can honestly say that the majority of men I was exposed to did not have those types of "God-like" qualities in them. As an impressionable young girl, I cannot say I felt prosperity and goodness vibrating through them to the point where it spilled over and impacted me or anyone else around them. I don't know about you, but that was not my experience.

The men I saw as a child growing up were not the type of men who made it a point to demonstrate King-like qualities to their wives and children. If anything—and this may be cultural for me as my family is from the Caribbean—the men desired to be served as though they were God. Moreover, they never made it a point to pour themselves into their wives and children, not in a manner that would display prosperity and divine goodness.

The majority of the men—not all—I was exposed to were dishonest, territorial, womanizers, cheaters, alcoholics, abusers, absentee dads, liars—and the list goes on and on. I always thought it was a cultural thing, like that's just what older Haitian men do. However, as I got older, I realized it wasn't only Haitian men; it was all men. Your race, background, skin color, and religious beliefs, do not designate whether or not you are going to be a good human being to the people around you.

The men I saw in my community growing up did not have the character that demonstrated responsibility, purpose, and vision. They did not elevate their sons to be fully mature men who could be decisive, authoritative, and impressive, and they damn sure didn't do that for their daughters. As I look back, I can maybe count on one hand the men who were in my community who were considered powerful men who were loved, revered, and respected as leaders of their household.

Never did I see the King in them. I never saw the man who took responsibility for his purpose in this world, created a vision for his life and manifested it beautifully and powerfully. As a young girl growing up, that was not my reality!

As I got older and became a woman in my fullness, I realized that I was not alone. After having countless conversations with colleagues, friends, acquaintances, and clients, I realized that there seems to be a shortage of men in our society who have fully manifested themselves as King. Once I delved into my studies and investigated more, I came to the tragic realization that many men in our society will die without ever reaching King status. Now, I want you to stop and think about what I just said...Many men in our society today will die and never, EVER reach King status.

I don't mean men who are killed and lose their lives prematurely. I'm speaking to the older men who've lived long lives who've never allowed their highest selves to emerge. Out of all four archetypes, this one appears to be the one that is under attack the most.

You may be asking yourself why I would say such a thing, and my response to you is that it doesn't take a rocket scientist to figure this out if you look around the world. Our world is off and unbalanced. We lack leadership and compassion toward one another. You can see it in our government, our politics, our policies as well as in our families... It's sad to say, but the wisdom of the strong grandfather or the strong father is rare nowadays. It is a sad state of affairs when we as a people have very few sovereign leaders.

Let's look at the media; it's doing a phenomenal job of emasculating men. Times have also changed such that now there is also a lack of clarity in gender roles, the lines between the sexes and their roles in society blurring and muddying, which further deteriorates the persona of the masculine male. But, Kings still exist; we just have to know how to find them and what this personality type brings to the table for us as women.

When it comes to the state of affairs with the modern-day man, let's start at the root cause; our boys! Our boys, our young men, are under attack. It's vital for our boys and young men to learn how to be a man from a man. I know many women who feel differently and disagree, but the truth remains that it takes a man to teach a young man how to become one.

Some men don't have a paternal bone in their body and have no business trying to be anyone's father. They are in their children's lives but feel as though providing a roof over their heads and putting food on the table is enough to show that they love them. That alone is not enough to adequately display the truth about manhood either.

One of the most beautiful sights to see is when a man takes interest in his son, when he takes the time to love him and nurture him so that he can evolve into a mature man who isn't afraid to be nurturing and caring to his own children when the time comes, for this is how kingship gets passed on from father to son, from generation to generation.

Sadly, there is an alarming number of men in our society today who are the products of absentee fathers. If you're a woman who is a single mom and is raising a son or sons, by no means am I saying you have to stay in a toxic relationship for the sake of your children. What I am saying is that just because you may no longer be together as a couple doesn't negate the fact that the man, the father, has a responsibility to ensure that his son is ushered appropriately into manhood. Families where the father is absent don't only impact the son for the years that he's growing up; it also affects his future relationships, his ability to show up powerfully for his own children one day and how he sees himself in the world. When men aren't involved in their son's life to teach him how to become a mature, masculine, Sovereign man, everyone pays the price.

In my world of relationship coaching, nine times out of ten, women find challenges with men who are lacking the embodiment of a King. Sadly, if we, as a society, don't get it together, the degradation of the clean and optimal manliness in its King form will be passed down from generation to generation instead of the true King archetype.

Chapter Fourteen: The Man Who Healthily Wears the Crown

The sovereign archetype, King, is a complete and holistic balance of the mature masculine Lover, Warrior, and Magician. If you think back to all the information I've shared with you up until this point, you remember that the ideal man is a man who has a healthy balance of the previously mentioned three archetypes. Let's consider Lover. A man who has a healthy balance of Lover can show up for you in a powerful way and meet your emotional, physical, and sexual needs. The Lover has the ability to leave you feeling loved, wanted, adored, lusted after, and appreciated. This archetype best meets all of a woman's emotional needs. So, if you take the mature Lover and you add the seasoned Warrior, whose role is to provide for and protect you and make sure you want for nothing in life, you're almost there. The Mature Magician, a man who is grounded in his sense of self, who knows who he is and has the intellectual capacity to thrive at work and within the intellectual community, will only add to their ideal man's qualities. A healthy combination of all three archetypes is King.

So, ladies, if you find yourself with a man who can show you deep, unwavering love, strong provision and protection, and is intellectually smart and stimulating, you've got yourself a keeper!

It Takes A Mature Man to Become King

The King in a man typically shows up later in his life. It's usually the last archetype to make itself present, because the other three archetypes must fully emerge and mature before they can meld together into one healthy King archetype. It's important to note that, because it's unlikely that you'll find a man fresh out of college, in his early to mid-twenties, who's already ready to be King. A young man still has a lot of growing up to do; he still has many experiences to get under his belt, life lessons that still need to be learned.

A mature young man who has great intentions and a good head on his shoulders can still be a fantastic catch to a young woman. However, he will not yet be a King. Kings are cultivated. Kings are made. Kings are seasoned, molded, crystallized. A man who is King is not still trying to learn himself; he's not still trying to find himself. HE IS! And, to a King, that is all that matters.

A King Does Not Hustle the Reigns

The man who has mastered the archetype of King is ruling over his kingdom. He's not waiting for someone else to come and build his kingdom for him. He's not trying to hustle you to help him pay for his kingdom. He is not looking for people to give him handouts to maintain his kingdom. No. A man is not yet a King until his kingdom is built and established on his own. I don't know about you, but in all of my years on this planet, I have yet to come across a king without a kingdom–one that he is leading. He is not a king for the sake of being called the King—or because he's good looking, a great lover, a wild dresser, or a sweet talker. He is a King because he embodies the personality traits and takes the actions of one.

A lot of men out here are of the right mindset when it comes to building their kingdom, but they haven't yet been able to achieve it. The kingdom is his home; the kingdom is his business. The kingdom is his legacy. Ask yourself if the man in your life has established those yet. Has he mastered that aspect of life? Is he in control of his own destiny within his own kingdom?

One of the best ways for you to determine if you have a king in your life is to notice whether he displays an inability to be comfortable within chaos. Is he comfortable taming and correcting any surprise situations that may fall onto his path? Kings do not allow chaos to overtake their kingdoms. The primary role of the King is to ensure that there is order. So, if you have a man in your life who does not do well with chaos—who panics or throws tantrums, who is unable to figure his own way out of difficult situations or is completely reliant on your help in order to do so —then he definitely is not demonstrating King-like tendencies and isn't yet ready for that title.

The King Treats His Queen as His Equal

Do you want to know if you have a King in your life? One of the best ways to determine this is by considering how he treats you.

A King is evolved enough to know there should be equality in the relationship. A man who has a healthy balance of the King archetype will not exert himself in a manner that shows supremacy or dominance over his Queen. The reason this is important to note is that a great King will live by the same governing principles he expects everyone else in his kingdom to abide by. So, if the kingdom is your household, then there needs to be equality that is established between the King and the Queen, or husband and wife. Neither party should exert force or control over the other. Any relationship that does not have equality between spouses is an indication that there are serious red flags that need to be addressed, immediately.

Leaving A Legacy

When a man has achieved King status, what drives him is no longer the conquest or acquisition. The continuity of his kingdom is what's most important to him. In addition to that, he wants to make sure that he is leaving his legacy in capable hands. Knowing that he has left his imprint on the planet so that the people he loves who come behind him are better off because of him is the ultimate goal of the King. This indicates he has lived a good and complete life.

A King's legacy is fundamentally grounded in how he interprets his identity, coupled with what he values. It means he takes responsibility for not only himself but his future children and their children, and he sets an example of accountability to them so that they can do the same for their children as well.

Legacy is evident in the man who has become King.

Chapter Fifteen: The Shadow Side of King

The Tyrant

The Tyrant hates, fears, and envies new life. He hates anything that represents his replacement as King. The Tyrant is the negatively inflated ego of a man fused with the power of a King.

Think of countries around the world that are being led by dictators. These particular leaders who lead with the Tyrant archetype do not welcome the idea, concept, or even the suggestion of a successor. They will label themselves as king for life, president for life, ruler for life.

You also see evidence of that in men who have strained relationships with their sons. This is because they view their sons as their replacement. There is an element of toxicity that is hardwired into their psyche when it comes to having a successor. When it comes to being in a relationship, as long as the woman does not present herself as a threat in regards to taking his throne or his position in any way, he's okay. But if the woman in his life elevates to the point where she becomes a threat to his supremacy, his Tyrant archetype will be activated.

How Do you Know if You're Dealing with a Tyrant?

- He becomes violent when presented with a threat to his supremacy It's imperative to his ego that he's seen as the absolute ruler.

- He may try to show love with grandiose gestures, but he still has a tendency of taking advantage of his woman.

- He can often become paranoid, abusive, and irrational toward others, often justifying his actions of abuse as righteous and just and as coming from a place of love.

- He will elevate himself above all, because he is his own priority.

- He must be seen, praised, worshiped, and admired. If not, he loses all sense of self, because he has attached his identity to being the King.

One thing to be mindful of is that often the Tyrant will view himself as a guide and will see nothing wrong with it. He also will expect you to revere him as though he is a God, and as his lover or the woman in his life, he expects you to worship him.

The Weakling

The other polar opposite of the male archetype, King, is the Weakling. The Weakling is a shell of a man. The man who leads with the Weakling archetype lacks calmness, centeredness, and security within himself. In my estimation, this is probably one of the worst archetype personas to be in a relationship with. Nothing is worse than being with a man who is unable to make decisions for himself, especially when you're looking to him to be confident and self-assured and take his role as a King seriously.

The Weakling King is a passive, deflated shell of a man who has handed over his sovereign power to others, even so far as allowing someone, or people, to take his power away from him. He willingly relinquishes his power, his responsibility, authority, and control over his life, taking comfort in knowing that he's accepted as being incapable of being the King. We often see this manifested as a man who passively allows his family to make all of his decisions for him, no matter how big or small. Though he has established a kingdom, a home, a family and even a business, he allows others to run it for him.

Being in a marriage or relationship can be extremely difficult with the Weakling. Not only is he weak, and he knows it, but he also targets people he perceives as more vulnerable than he is with what may appear to be passive verbal attacks, because these attacks inflate his ego without forcing him to exert too much effort. It is disappointing to see how he takes pleasure in disempowering others for the sake of his ego. He is the complete antithesis of a King.

The Weakling is typically indicative of a man who was abused as a child and either did not or was not able to seek the proper help. That is an absolute necessity in order for him to mature and develop into a fully formed man who is grounded in being King. So, while he may display aspects of the Lover, the Warrior, and the Magician, he is unable to manifest them with positivity and vitality.

In summary, the Weakling is not the type of man you want to have or to be in a relationship with. As a woman who desires to either have a partnership or be led by a man, it's imperative and utterly crucial that you can trust your life as well as your children's lives in his hands. Whenever he is faced with threats, the Weakling exerts what little power he has in order to trample on someone weaker than he is, rather than using the same energy to build himself and his family up.

It's important to note that the King's objective is always clear. His role is to provide order, certainty, protection, and balance to his realm. Anything that is happening outside of his Kingdom is not of his concern, since his kingdom is clearly defined. A King knows he is not only living for himself. He fully understands that his existence is to ensure that all he's responsible for is loved and protected. A man who is King (the head of his household) is clear on his role in taking care of his family and makes sure their wellbeing is his priority. It is important for the King to know that his children are equipped and able to thrive when he is no longer around. He has the maturity to not need to put himself first. He has the confidence to know that one day he will transfer all that he has to his children and that they will be able to take the foundation he has provided for them to build upon for generations to come. Legacy is his purpose. A King with nothing to leave behind would feel that his life was in vain.

The King is the perfect balance of Lover, Warrior and Magician and don't let a man who is not a King convince you otherwise!

The Work

The work is a section at the conclusion of each archetype that allows you to take in what you read about the archetype and reflect on relationships you've had with a man or men who lead(s) with this archetype. Whether it's the positive side or the shadow side of his archetype, I want you to fully meditate on what you read and honor your process in growing what was shared. This page is being offered to you so that you can fully express how you feel about what you have learned and what enhancements you will make to your love life for the future.

This is your space to be honest and true to yourself. Here's a warning. Sometimes, self-discovery is not always pleasant. It can be an extremely bitter pill to swallow. But, what I can assure you of is this: If you are ready to learn and understand where you can make changes in the mistakes you have been making with the men you choose or if you come to the realization that the man in your life is truly who you want, then taking the time to do the work is priceless. Be gentle with yourself, trust your process, and know that this will take you closer to enlightenment and personal understanding.

1) After learning about the King, I realized...

2). What did you learn about yourself when it comes to re-lating to the King archetype in men?

3). Have you been in a relationship with a man who leads with one of the shadow sides of the King archetype? If yes, what clarity did you gain from this section of the book?

4). How will you better relate to men who lead with the King archetype?

ABOUT THE AUTHOR

Rachel Davis is a Master Confidence and Relationship Expert who specializes in helping high-powered, career-focused women win in love, so they can have the passion-filled and safe love life they desire. Rachel is masterful at teaching women how to hone in on and exude über femininity by tapping into their personal power and becoming comfortable with their feminine self.

As a Fortune 500 executive in a male-dominated industry, Rachel spent more than twenty years of her adult working career in the trenches of corporate America climbing that proverbial ladder, only to bump her head repeatedly against the glass ceiling. During her tenure in the cubicle jungle, she successfully leads teams, projects, and work initiatives without out ever compromising her femininity or diminishing her womanhood. Her experience has provided her with invaluable perspectives that enable her to be an effective leader, thoughtful communicator, coach, mentor, and a champion for women who are seeking to fulfill their purpose with confidence.

Rachel has not always been successful in love. With a failed marriage in her past, she was determined to learn from her past mistakes, heartache, and tears. When she found herself married for the second time, to the man of her dreams, she was determined to make this marriage work. Rachel went on a quest to learn all she could about men, and that is when "it" happened. "It" being a complete and thorough education around understanding "men." With that education, she became a powerful force in her marriage. Rachel was able to cultivate intimacy, passion, safe communication, deep understanding, mutual respect, honesty, trust, success, kindness, integrity, dependability, laughter, generosity, romance, faithfulness, and unconditional love. Once mastered, Rachel became determined to share what she'd learned with women all across the world.

Rachel is leading an entire generation of women from a stagnant place of mediocrity to a higher level of greatness, to be in tune with their highest self and to attract the man of their dreams all while creating an environment that will get his heart beating to her rhythm. Rachel's goal is to add more value to your world than you've ever dreamed possible. Her coaching and training strategies give you the tools you'll need to send your love life to new heights, thus creating radical change in your ability to make an impact in your love life, effortlessly connect with men, and manifest your confident self, all while falling in love with the person you'll become.

website: www.lovebyracheldavis.com

Made in the
USA
Lexington, KY